Also by Paul Fleischman

Poetry
Big Talk: Poems for Four Voices
Joyful Noise: Poems for Two Voices
I Am Phoenix: Poems for Two Voices

Picture Books
Sidewalk Circus
The Animal Hedge
Weslandia
Lost
Time Train

Novels
Breakout
Seek
Mind's Eye
Whirligig
Seedfolks
A Fate Totally Worse Than Death
Bull Run
The Borning Room
Saturnalia
The Half-a-Moon Inn

Nonfiction
Cannibal in the Mirror
Dateline: Troy

JOYFUL NOISE

Poems for Two Voices

JOYFUL NOISE
Poems for Two Voices

PAUL FLEISCHMAN
illustrated by Eric Beddows

A Charlotte Zolotow Book

HarperTrophy®
An Imprint of HarperCollins Publishers

Harper Trophy® is a registered trademark of
HarperCollins Publishers Inc.

Joyful Noise: Poems for Two Voices
Text copyright © 1988 by Paul Fleischman
Illustrations copyright © 1988 by Eric Beddows
Manufactured in China.

Library of Congress Cataloging-in-Publication Data
Fleischman, Paul.
    Joyful noise.
    "A Charlotte Zolotow Book."
    Summary: A collection of poems describing the characteristics and
activities of a variety of insects.
ISBN 0-06-021852-5 — ISBN 0-06-021853-3 (lib. bdg.)
ISBN 0-06-446093-2 (pbk.)
    1. Insects—Juvenile poetry. 2. Children's poetry, American. [1.
Insects—Poetry. 2. American poetry.] I. Beddows, Eric, 1951– ill. II.
Title.
PS3556.L42268J69 1988 811'.54   87-45280

Typography by Constance Fogler

For Seth, our porch light
P. F.

for E. H. and Echo Hill Farm with its
wonderful fireflies
E. B.

CONTENTS

Grasshoppers / 3

Water Striders / 5

Mayflies / 8

Fireflies / 11

Book Lice / 15

The Moth's Serenade / 18

Water Boatmen / 21

The Digger Wasp / 23

Cicadas / 26

Honeybees / 29

Whirligig Beetles / 32

Requiem / 34

House Crickets / 36

Chrysalis Diary / 39

NOTE

The following poems were written to be read aloud by
two readers at once, one taking the left-hand part, the other taking
the right-hand part. The poems should be read from top to bottom,
the two parts meshing as in a musical duet. When both readers
have lines at the same horizontal level, those lines
are to be spoken simultaneously.

JOYFUL NOISE
Poems for Two Voices

Grasshoppers

Sap's rising

Ground's warming

Grasshoppers are
hatching out
Autumn-laid eggs

Grasshoppers are
hatching out

splitting

Young stepping

into spring

Grasshoppers
hopping
high
Grassjumpers
jumping

Vaulting from
leaf to leaf
stem to stem
plant to plant

leapers
Grass-
bounders

springers
Grass-
soarers
Leapfrogging
longjumping
grasshoppers.

Grasshoppers
hopping

Grassjumpers
jumping
far

leaf to leaf
stem to stem
Grass-
leapers

bounders
Grass-
springers

soarers
Leapfrogging
longjumping
grasshoppers.

Water Striders

Whenever we're asked
if we walk upon water
we answer

To be sure.

Whenever we're asked
if we walk upon water
we answer
Of course.

It's quite true.

Whenever we're asked
if we walk on it often
we answer
Quite often.

All day through.
Should we be questioned
on whether it's easy
we answer

A snap.

Should we be told
that it's surely a miracle
we reply
Balderdash!

Nonsense!
Whenever we're asked
for instructions
we always say

and do as we do.

Whenever we're asked
if we walk on it often
we answer

Each day.

Should we be questioned
on whether it's easy
we answer
Quite easy.

It's a cinch.
Should we be told
that it's surely a miracle
we reply

Rubbish!

Whenever we're asked
for instructions
we always say
Come to the pond's edge

Put down one foot

and then put down another,

resting upon the thin film
on the surface.

Believe me, there's no call
at all to be nervous

as long as you're reasonably
mindful that you—

But by that time our student
no matter how prudent
has usually

But by that time our student

has usually
don't ask me why

sunk from view.

sunk from view.

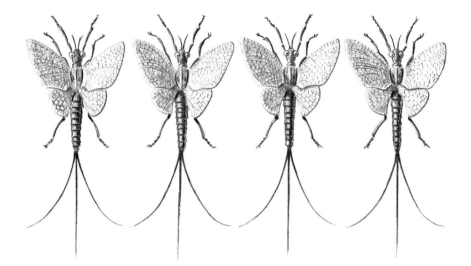

Mayflies

Your moment

        Mayfly month

Your hour

        Mayfly year

Your trifling day

        Our life

We're mayflies   We're mayflies

just emerging   just emerging

rising from the river,
born this day in May

and dying day,

this single sip of living

We're mayflies
by the millions
fevered

rushed

We're mayflies
swarming, swerving,
rising high

courting on the wing,

We're mayflies
laying eggs
our final, frantic act.

birthday

this particle of time

all that we're allowed.
We're mayflies
by the millions

frenzied

no redwood's centuries
to squander as we please.
We're mayflies
swarming, swerving,

then falling,

then mating in midair.
We're mayflies
laying eggs

(9)

Sun's low

light's weak

in haste we launch them
down the stream.

We're mayflies   We're mayflies
lying dying   lying dying
floating by the millions

                         on the very stream

from which we sprung
so very long ago

                         this morning
back when we were   back when we were
young.   young.

Fireflies

Light

Night
is our parchment

Light
is the ink we use

Night

We're
fireflies

fireflies
flitting

flickering

flashing

fireflies
glimmering

fireflies
gleaming

glowing
Insect calligraphers
practicing penmanship

Insect calligraphers

copying sentences

Six-legged scribblers
of vanishing messages,

Six-legged scribblers

fleeting graffiti

Fine artists in flight
adding dabs of light

Signing the June nights
as if they were paintings

flickering
fireflies
fireflies.

Fine artists in flight

bright brush strokes
Signing the June nights
as if they were paintings
We're
fireflies
flickering
fireflies.

Book Lice

I was born in a
fine old edition of Schiller

       While I started life
       in a private eye thriller

We're book lice   We're book lice
who dwell   who dwell
in these dusty bookshelves.   in these dusty bookshelves.
Later I lodged in
Scott's works—volume 50

       While I passed my youth
       in an Agatha Christie

We're book lice
attached
despite contrasting pasts.
One day, while in search of
a new place to eat

We're book lice
who chew
on the bookbinding glue.
We honeymooned in an
old guide book on Greece

We're book lice
attached
despite contrasting pasts.

He fell down seven shelves,
where we happened to meet

We're book lice
who chew
on the bookbinding glue.

                                    I missed Conan Doyle,
                                    he pined for his Keats

We're book lice   We're book lice
fine mates   fine mates
despite different tastes.   despite different tastes.
So we set up our home
inside Roget's Thesaurus

                                    Not far from my mysteries,
                                    close to his Horace

We're book lice   We're book lice
adoring   adoring
despite her loud snoring.   despite his loud snoring.
And there we've resided,
and there we'll remain,

                                    He nearby his Shakespeare,
                                    I near my Spillane

We're book-loving   We're book-loving
book lice   book lice
                                    plain proof of the fact

which I'm certain I read
in a book some months back
that opposites   that opposites
often are known   often are known
to attract.   to attract.

The Moth's Serenade

Porch
light,
hear my plight!
I drink your light
like nectar

by day
Gaze in your eyes
all night
Porch light!

Porch
light,
hear my plight!

like nectar
Dream of you
by day

all night
Porch light!

I am
your seeking
circling
sighing
lovesick
knight
You are

my soul's
desire
my prize

Porch light!
My shining star!

"Keep back," they say
I can't!
"Don't touch," they say

Porch light!
Let's clasp
Let's kiss
Let's marry for a trice!

Bright paradise!
I am

seeking
circling
sighing

You are
my soul's
desire
my prize
my eyes'
delight

Porch light!

My compass needle's North!

"Keep back," they say

"Don't touch," they say
I must!

Porch light!
Let's kiss
Let's clasp
Let's marry for a trice!

Porch light!   Porch light!

Let's meet   Let's merge

Let's merge   Let's meet

Let's live for love!

For light!   For light!

Water Boatmen

"Stroke!"
We're water boatmen
"Stroke!"

"Stroke!"
We're cockswain calling
"Stroke!"

"Stroke!"

"Stroke!"

"Stroke!"
up early, rowing
"Stroke!"

"Stroke!"
and oarsmen straining
"Stroke!"

and six-man racing shell
rolled into one.

We're water boatmen

"Stroke!"   "Stroke!"
worn-out from rowing
"Stroke!"

                             "Stroke!"
                             Bound for the bottom
"Stroke!"   "Stroke!"
of this deep millpond
"Stroke!"

                             "Stroke!"
                             where we arrive
and shout the order
"Rest!"   "Rest!"

The Digger Wasp

I will never
see my children,

they will never
gaze on me.

I'll have died

when they're emerging
next July.
So it must be.

So it must be.

Yet, when they
behold the home

I'm digging now
for their protection,

safe and snug

far underground,
they'll recognize
my deep affection.

they'll recognize
my deep affection.
When they hatch
and find a caterpillar,

stung and paralyzed,

left by me

for them to eat
they'll know as well
that I was wise.

they'll know as well
that I was wise.
When they learn
I'd dragged it there

in spite of every
interference,

weeds and rocks

and thieving beetles,
they'll discern
my perseverance.

they'll discern
my perseverance.
While, cocooned,

they pass the winter

safe from snow
and ice and chill,

they'll perceive

and thank me for
my formidable
digging skill.

my formidable
digging skill.
By the time they're
ready, next July,

to climb up from their cells

and break the burrow's seal

and fly away
my young will
know me well.

my young will
know me well.
When they care
for their own children,

never to be looked upon,

they'll feel my love

in replica
and know that they, in turn,
were cherished

in replica

by the mother digger wasp
whose face and form
they never saw.

whose face and form
they never saw.

(25)

Cicadas

Afternoon, mid-August
Two cicadas singing

Two cicadas singing
Air kiln-hot, lead-heavy

Five cicadas humming
Five cicadas humming
Thunderheads northwestward

Twelve cicadas buzzing
Twelve cicadas buzzing
Up and down the street

the mighty choir's
assembling

the mighty choir's
assembling

Shrill cica-
das
droning

         Ci-
         cadas
         droning
         in the elms

Three years
spent underground

         Three years

         among the roots
in darkness   in darkness
Now they're breaking ground

         and climbing up
         the tree trunks

splitting skins
and singing   and singing
         Jubilant
rejoicing   cicadas
         pouring out their
fervent praise   fervent praise
         for heat and light
their hymn   their hymn
sung to the sun
Cicadas   Cicadas
         whining

whin-
ing   ci-
                                       cadas
                                       whirring

whir-
ring   ci-
                                       cadas
                                       pulsing

pulsing
chanting from the treetops   chanting from the treetops
sending
forth their   sending
booming   forth their
boisterous   booming
joyful noise!   joyful noise!

Honeybees

Being a bee

is a pain.

I'm a worker
I'll gladly explain.

I'm up at dawn, guarding
the hive's narrow entrance

Being a bee
is a joy.

I'm a queen

I'll gladly explain.
Upon rising, I'm fed
by my royal attendants,

                    I'm bathed

then I take out
the hive's morning trash

                    then I'm groomed.

then I put in an hour
making wax,
without two minutes' time
to sit still and relax.

                    The rest of my day
                    is quite simply set forth:

Then I might collect nectar
from the field
three miles north

                    I lay eggs,

or perhaps I'm on
larva detail

                    by the hundred.

feeding the grubs
in their cells,
wishing that *I* were still
helpless and pale.

                    I'm loved and I'm lauded,
                    I'm outranked by none.

Then I pack combs with
pollen—not my idea of fun.

                    When I've done
                    enough laying

Then, weary, I strive

                    I retire

to patch up any cracks
in the hive.

                    for the rest of the day.

Then I build some new cells,
slaving away at
enlarging this Hell,
dreading the sight
of another sunrise,
wondering why we don't
all unionize.

Truly, a bee's is the   Truly, a bee's is the
worst   best
of all lives.   of all lives.

Whirligig Beetles

We're whirligig beetles
we're swimming in circles,
black backs by the hundred.

We're spinning and swerving
as if we were on a
mad merry-go-round.
We never get dizzy
from whirling and weaving
and wheeling and swirling.

We're whirligig beetles
we're swimming in circles,
black backs by the hundred.
We're spinning and swerving
as if we were on a
mad merry-go-round.

We never get dizzy
from whirling and weaving
and wheeling and swirling.
The same goes for turning,

The same goes for turning,
revolving and curving,
gyrating and twirling.
The crows fly directly,
but we prefer spirals,
arcs, ovals, and loops.

"As the whirligig swims"

circular
roundabout
backtracking
indirect
serpentine
tortuous
twisty,
best possible
route.

revolving and curving,
gyrating and twirling.

The crows fly directly,
but we prefer spirals,
arcs, ovals, and loops.
We're fond of the phrase
"As the whirligig swims"
meaning traveling by
the most circular

roundabout
backtracking
indirect
serpentine
tortuous
twisty and
turny,
best possible
route.

Requiem

Grant them rest eternal
Maple moths
Let light undying
shine upon them.

green darners
rest eternal

Carolina sphinx moths
Grant them rest eternal

Let light undying
shine upon them.
Praying mantises

rest eternal

brown darners
light undying.
Grasshoppers
great crested

three-banded
Katydids

northern

Cave crickets
mole crickets
tree crickets
field crickets

rest eternal

light undying.
This past night
we had the fall's first
killing frost.

Black-winged damselflies

light undying.
Grasshoppers

spur-throated

Katydids
round-headed

gladiator

Cave crickets
mole crickets
tree crickets
Grant them
rest eternal
Give them
light undying.

House Crickets

We don't live in meadows

crick-et   crick-et

or in groves

We're house crickets

living beneath

this gas stove

crick-et   crick-et

Others may worry

crick-et
about fall

crick-et

We're scarcely aware
of the seasons at all

crick-et
Spring, to house crickets,

crick-et

crick-et
means no more

crick-et

than the time
when fresh greens
once again grace the floor

crick-et
Summer's the season

crick-et

crick-et
for pie crumbs:

crick-et

peach, pear, boysenberry,
quince, apricot, plum

crick-et
Pumpkin seeds tell us

crick-et

crick-et
fall's arrived

crick-et

while hot chocolate spills
hint that it's
winter outside.

No matter the month
we stay well fed and warm,

No matter the month

unconcerned about cold fronts
and wind chill and storms.

For while others are ruled
by the sun in the heavens,

For while others are ruled

whose varying height brings
the seasons' procession,

we live in a world
of fixed Fahrenheit
crick-et

we live in a world

crick-et
thanks to *our* sun:

our unchanging

reliable

steadfast and stable
bright blue
pilot light.

bright blue
pilot light.

Chrysalis Diary

November 13:

Cold told me
to fasten my feet
to this branch,

to dangle upside down
from my perch,

to shed my skin,

to cease being a caterpillar
and I have obeyed.

and I have obeyed.

December 6:

        Green,

the color of leaves and life,

has vanished!

        has vanished!

        The empire of leaves

lies in ruins!

        lies in ruins!

I study the

brown new world around me.

        I fear the future.

I hear few sounds.

        Have any others of my kind

        survived this cataclysm?

Swinging back and forth

in the wind,

I feel immeasurably alone.

        January 4:

I can make out snow falling.

        For five days and nights

        it's been drifting down.

I find I never tire of

watching the flakes

in their multitudes

passing my window.

Astounding.
I enter these
wondrous events
in my chronicle

The world is now white.
Astounding.

knowing no reader
would believe me.

February 12:

An ice storm last night.

Unable to see out
at all this morning.

Yet I hear boughs cracking

and branches falling.

Hungry for sounds
in this silent world,
I cherish these,

ponder their import,

miser them away
in my memory,

and wait for more.

and wait for more.

March 28:

I wonder whether
I am the same being
who started this diary.

I've felt stormy inside

like the weather without.

My mouth is reshaping,

my legs are dissolving,

wings are growing

my body's not mine.
This morning,
a breeze from the south,
strangely fragrant,

my body's not mine.

a red-winged blackbird's
call in the distance,

a faint glimpse of green
in the branches.

And now I recall
that last night
I dreamt of flying.